You're Wearing That to School?!

BY
Lynn Plourde

ILLUSTRATED BY
Sue Cornelison

DISNEY • HYPERION BOOKS / NEW YORK

6/13

First Edition
10 9 8 7 6 5 4 3 2 1
G615-7693-2-13074
Printed in China

Library of Congress Cataloging-in-Publication Data
Plourde, Lynn
You're wearing that to school?! / by Lynn Plourde ; illustrated by Sue Cornelison.—1st ed.
p. cm.
Summary: A cautious mouse named Tiny gives advice to his best friend, an exuberant hippopotamus named
Penelope, on such things as what to wear and what to take for show-and-tell on the first day of school.
ISBN 978-1-4231-5510-2 (hardcover)
[1. First day of school—Fiction. 2. Schools—Fiction. 3. Individuality—Fiction.
4. Hippopotamus—Fiction. 5. Mice—Fiction.]
I. Cornelison, Sue, ill. II. Title. III. Title: You are wearing that to school?!
PZ7.P724Yo 2013 [E]—dc23 2011031614

Reinforced binding
Visit www.disneyhyperionbooks.com

To Addie, who's already a fashionista
—L.P.

For my daughters, Marissa Rae and Molly Catherine,
whose creative spirit is a joy to behold
—S.C.

Penelope

did her

happy hippo

dance.

"Watch where you step!"
squeaked Tiny.
"Don't worry," said Penelope.
"I wouldn't squish my best friend."

"Why the good mood?" asked Tiny.
Penelope climbed up a tree and proclaimed,

"School!
The first day of school is tomorrow!"

"Oh, *that*," Tiny groaned.
"Yes!" said Penelope. "Lucky *you* started
school last year. Now it's *my* turn."
Tiny grumbled, "Starting school
is tricky."

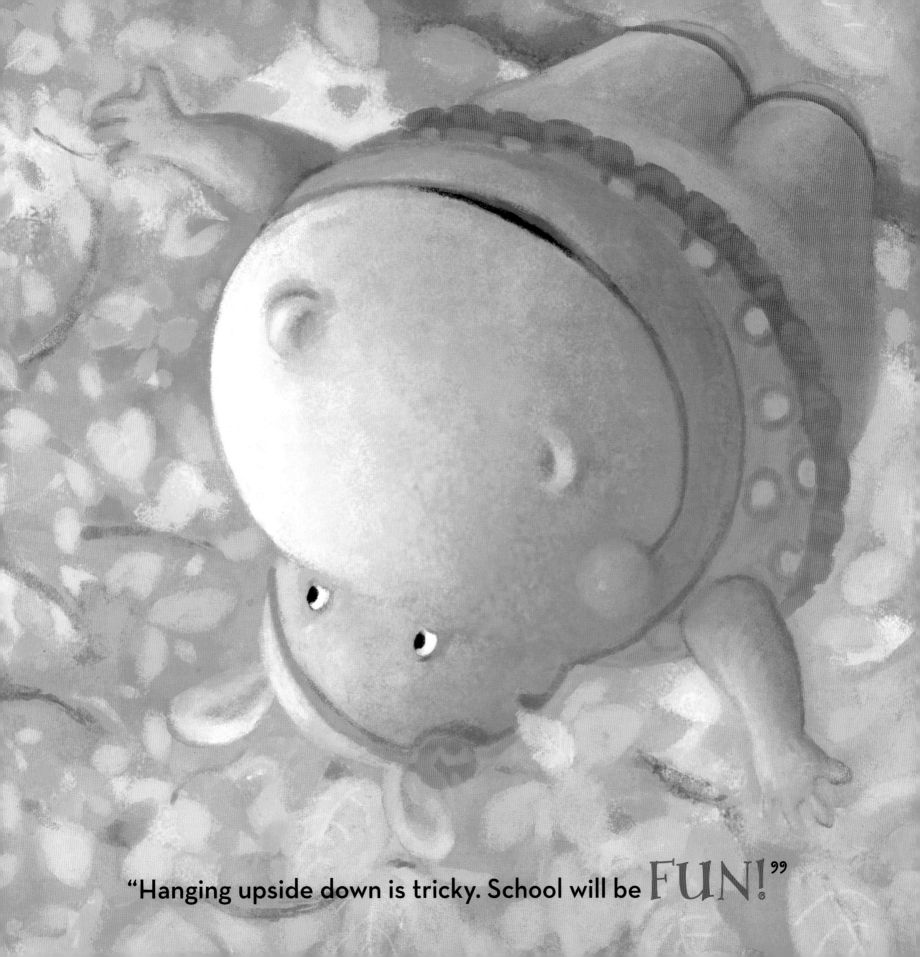

"Hanging upside down is tricky. School will be FUN!"

"Oh, Penelope, you have so much to learn." Tiny sighed.

"Like what?"

"Like clothes! What will you wear the first day?"

"No problem." Penelope smiled. "I'll wear my sparkle rainbow outfit."

"You're going to wear **THAT?**" Tiny asked.
"Yes! It's my favorite." Penelope giggled.
"Everyone will stare. Come on." Tiny tugged.
"I'll help you find a perfect outfit."

"Oh, yes!" said Penelope.

"Oh, no!"
said Tiny.

"Plain?" asked Penelope.
"Perfect," said Tiny. "You'll fit right in."

"Guess I'm ready now," said Penelope.
"Thanks, Tiny."
"Not so fast," Tiny said. "What are you
going to bring for lunch tomorrow?"
"No problem." Penelope smiled.

"I'll pack a picnic."

"You're going to eat **THAT**?"
"Yes! I love picnics."
"What will everyone think?
Come on." Tiny tugged. "I'll help
you pack a perfect lunch."

"Peanut butter and jelly?
How ordinary," said Penelope.
"That's the point," said Tiny.
"Just like everyone else's."

"Thanks, Tiny! Now I'm ready for the BIG day tomorrow."
"Maybe," said Tiny. "What about show-and-tell?"

"No problem." Penelope smiled.
"I'm going to bring Hugsy Hippo."

"You're going to bring **THAT**?"

"Yes! I've had it since I was a baby. My grammy made it for me," said Penelope.

"Big kids don't bring baby things to school. Come on." Tiny tugged. "I'll help you find something perfect for show-and-tell."

"Oh, yes!"
said Penelope.

"Oh, no!"
said Tiny.

"Oh, yes, yes!"
said Penelope.

"Oh, no, no!"
said Tiny.

"A plain old rock? Ho hum," said Penelope.

"Rocks are the most popular show-and-tell item," explained Tiny. "Kids just pick them up on the way to school."

"Thanks, Tiny. You're right—starting school is tricky."

"And tiring," agreed Tiny. "I'll see you tomorrow at the bus stop."

Morning arrived. Penelope did her
happy hippo dance.

Then she got dressed and packed her
backpack.

When she arrived at the bus stop,
Tiny was already there.

"Where's your new outfit?" asked Tiny.

"I like this sparkle rainbow one, after all,"
said Penelope.

Tiny eyed Penelope's backpack. "You didn't
listen to a word I said, did you?" Tiny saw all
the other kids staring at them.

The bus pulled up.

"May I sit with you?" asked Penelope.

Tiny looked around. "Um . . ."

Penelope shrugged. "It's okay if you don't want me to."

"Just watch where you sit!"
squeaked Tiny as he moved over.
"Don't worry. I wouldn't squish
my best friend."

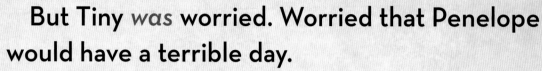

But Tiny *was* worried. Worried that Penelope would have a terrible day.

She didn't know how tricky school could be.

The bell rang, and they headed off to their different classrooms.

Penelope and Tiny met outside the lunch room at noon.

"You did it!" Tiny gave Penelope a low five. "You survived your first morning at school."

"Oh, yes!" said Penelope.

"Come on," said Tiny. "Let's find a table with room for two."

"Oh, no, no!" said Penelope, opening the door.

They wouldn't see each other again until lunchtime. Tiny hoped Penelope wouldn't be too lonely.

TIPS FOR A Hippo Happy FIRST DAY OF SCHOOL

❊ In your backpack, bring a favorite thing of yours from home.
You don't have to take it out. Just knowing it's there will make you feel better.

❊ Plan to connect with a friend sometime during the day.
Maybe on the bus, at recess, during lunch, whenever you can.

❊ If you don't know anyone else at school, don't panic. There will be other kids who don't know anyone. You're all just friends who haven't met yet.
Go up to someone who's alone and say something friendly.

❊ Familiar food is a good idea on the first day.
Whether you bring food from home or have hot lunch, choose something you *know* you like. You can try new foods on other days.

❊ Wear clothes on the first day that follow the Goldilocks rule.
You don't want clothes that are too scratchy, too warm, too loose, or too tight. Only wear clothes that are . . . JUST RIGHT!

❊ If the first day of school isn't perfect, don't worry.
There's always the second day, the third day, the fourth day. . . .